Under the Official Secrets Act 1989, Chapter 6, subsection 1, a person who is or has been:

    (a) a member of the security and intelligence services; or

    (b) notified that he is subject to the provisions of this subsection

is guilty of an offense if without lawful authority he discloses any information, document, or other article relating to security or intelligence that is or has been in his possession by virtue of his position as a member of any of those services or in the course of his work while the notification is or was in force.

I hereby agree to abide by the provisions of the Act.

Signature_____ Date_____

All photographs © Science Photo Library and individuals as credited below:

p.8, Volker Steger; p.11, Sheila Terry; p.12 left, Andrew Lambert Photography; p.12 right, Jim Stoots, Lawrence Livermore National Laboratory; p.14, Martyn F. Chillmaid; p.15, Alfred Pasieka; p.16, Sandia National Laboratories; p.17, Sidney Moulds; p.19, Dr. Peter Harris; p.20 left, Chris Knapton; p.20 right, Lawrence Lawry; p.22 left, Dr. Gary Settles; p.22 right, Charles D. Winters; p.24 left, Alexander Tsiaras; p.24 right, Mehau Kulyk; p.26, Dr. Tony Brain; p.27, American Science & Engineering; p.29, Dr. Jeremy Burgess; p.30, Geoff Williams; p.31, Philippe Plailly; p.32, Geoff Tompkinson; p.34, Science Photo Library; p.35, Jerry Mason; p.36, Dale Boyer; p.38 left, Charles D. Winters; p.38 right, Tom McHugh; p.41, Gusto; p.42, Victor Habbick Visions.

PHILOMEL BOOKS

A division of Penguin Young Readers Group.

Published by The Penguin Group.

Penguin Group (USA) Inc., 375 Hudson Street, New York, NY 10014, U.S.A.

Penguin Group (Canada), 90 Eglinton Avenue East, Suite 700, Toronto, Ontario, Canada M4P 2Y3 (a division of Pearson Penguin Canada Inc.)

Penguin Books Ltd, 80 Strand, London WC2R ORL, England.

Penguin Ireland, 25 St. Stephen's Green, Dublin 2, Ireland (a division of Penguin Books Ltd.)

Penguin Group (Australia), 250 Camberwell Road, Camberwell, Victoria 3124, Australia (a division of Pearson Australia Group Pty Ltd).

Penguin Books India Pvt Ltd, 11 Community Centre, Panchsheel Park, New Delhi - 110 017, India.

Penguin Group (NZ), Cnr Airborne and Rosedale Roads, Albany, Auckland 1310, New Zealand (a division of Pearson New Zealand Ltd).

Penguin Books (South Africa) (Pty) Ltd, 24 Sturdee Avenue, Rosebank, Johannesburg 2196, South Africa.

Penguin Books Ltd, Registered Offices: 80 Strand, London WC2R ORL, England.

Text copyright © 2005 by Anthony Horowitz. Illustration copyright © 2005 by John Lawson.

Alex Rider Icon™ © 2005 by Walker Books Ltd. First published in 2005 by Walker Books Ltd, London.

Published simultaneously in Canada. Printed in China.

The illustrations are computer generated.

Library of Congress Cataloging-in-Publication Data is available upon request.

L.C. Number: 2005049622.

ISBN 0-399-24486-7

10 9 8 7 6 5 4 3

ANTHONY HOROWITZ

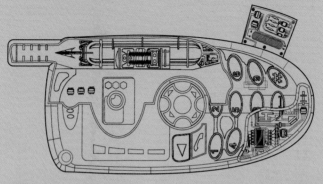

ALEX RIDER
THE GADGETS

TECHNICAL RESEARCHER: Emil Fortune

TECHNICAL ILLUSTRATOR: John Lawson

PHILOMEL BOOKS

Introduction

From: Smithers (Covert Weapons Section)
To: Alan Blunt (CE Special Operations, MI6)
Subject: Dossier

I have received your request for a breakdown of all devices used by Alex Rider on his first five missions.

If I may say so, and with the greatest respect, I am rather baffled. What is it, I wonder, that you wish to do with this dossier? I need hardly remind you of the trouble with dossiers that we at MI6 have had in the past!

I am very concerned that the hard work undertaken by my department may fall into the wrong hands. Organizations such as Scorpia (to name but one) would have a keen interest in knowing what we get up to here. But even our American friends in the CIA have made no secret of their desire to see our blueprints—simply so they can appropriate them.

If you are going to produce a book of some sort, I would suggest we build in a simple device that will cause it to burst into flames when it is opened. I used just such a trick in a get-well card that I sent Alex when he was in the hospital after his last mission. I'm told he liked it very much, although the nurses and fire brigade were perhaps less amused.

Or might you at least consider publishing the dossier in code? A simple code such as this, for example:

1L2 XR3 D2R 3S1 S5P 2RB 4P2 R1T 3V2

Anyway, it is now almost a year since you told me that we might have a fourteen-year-old agent joining us. I have to say, I nearly ate my hat—not difficult, in fact, as it was manufactured to produce emergency rations in the field. As you requested, however, I began to think of covert weapons (we do insist on calling them "gadgets"—although I've always found the word inappropriate, myself) which might be of use.

This provided a very interesting challenge. You will be familiar with some of our recent successes. The exploding briefcase, X-ray video camera, semiautomatic golf clubs, and toxic aftershave have all become standard issue. I am particularly proud of the Palm Organizer which we converted to become a miniature flame-thrower. You will recall that we renamed this the Napalm Organizer.

But all of these are only really suitable for adults and you were asking me to equip a fourteen-year-old boy! And so, when I began devising weapons for Alex Rider, I had to start with this question. What would a teenager be likely to have in his pockets—apart, that is, from his hands? It is fortunate that I have a nephew of the same age as Alex and was able to take a quick peek in his bedroom—this gave me the inspiration for the devices that you will find described on the pages that follow.

My nephew has at one time or another owned a handheld games console, a yo-yo, a tube of zit cream, a bicycle, a Harry Potter novel (although I'm afraid he never finished it), a personal CD player, a cellular phone, and a pack of bubble gum. I have managed to turn all of these everyday objects into serviceable weapons.

I wonder, by the way, if you might ever consider sending a young female agent into action? I have, for example, developed a very pretty doll that cries, wets itself, and then blows up. My department is also working on a bracelet where every item on the chain produces a different toxic gas when dissolved in water. Not so much a charm bracelet as a harm bracelet, we like to think.

One very tricky problem we have had to confront is your insistence that all Alex's weapons should be nonlethal. For example, when we sent Alex to Skeleton Key, he was equipped with a model five cell phone (the antenna was actually a stun dart that could be fired at a range of up to sixty feet) rather than the far more dangerous model seven, which blows up when you dial unless it is held upside down. This model is known as a "hands free," as many enemy agents who have tried to use it have indeed found themselves free of any hands.

Another example is the key ring that Alex used to escape from General Sarov at Edinburgh Airport. Like the model five phone, this device contained a fairly harmless stun grenade instead of something more dangerous. The enemy was knocked out but recovered all too quickly, and as a result Alex was recaptured.

My Rubik's Cube hand grenade was also rejected by you, you may remember, although I admit that this was not one of my department's greatest successes, as you had to line up all the colors to arm the thing, which could take days.

Nonetheless, I have to say that I am puzzled by your attitude. I hardly need remind you that Alex has confronted some of the most dangerous criminals in the world. Herod Sayle, Dr. Grief, General Sarov, Damian Cray—none of them would think twice before killing him. Most of them, in fact, wouldn't think once. But he is only ever allowed to knock them out!

I know Alex is a juvenile. But he has always struck me as being a very levelheaded boy . . . the sort of boy who would never strike anyone, in fact, except in self-defense. I have spoken to the Armory Section and they are also keen to equip him. They have suggested a third-generation 9mm Smith & Wesson, for example. Something simple to get him started. Can we discuss this at our next interdepartmental meeting?

For your interest, I have included some of the weaponry that was not developed by my department. The Geiger counter games console, for example, was created by the CIA. To my mind, our own Geiger counter (concealed in an electric toothbrush) is more effective. But it's revealing to know what our associates are up to.

For the same reason, I have outlined several of the devices invented by Scorpia. I was particularly struck by the fake pizza that Alex was given. Actually, it's lucky I wasn't struck by it as the thermite charges disguised as olives could have been deadly. They also found an ingenious way to conceal a Kahr P9 double-action semiautomatic in a bottle of soft drink.

There is no doubt that Scorpia scientists—in particular the late Dr. Liebermann—came within an inch of killing many thousands of children in London. We need to look more closely at the whole, terrifying world of nanotechnology.

It has been a very rare pleasure and a privilege to prepare Alex Rider for his first five missions and, although I do worry about the boy, you can be assured that I and my department will continue to do everything in our power to keep him safe.

Smithers

Contents

Cutter CD Player

When Alex was sent to infiltrate the mysterious Point Blanc Academy, gadgets were a problem. The only piece of electronic equipment Alex was allowed to take was a personal CD player—as long as all his CDs were classical! So Smithers' CD player works just like the real thing—except for two important secret features.

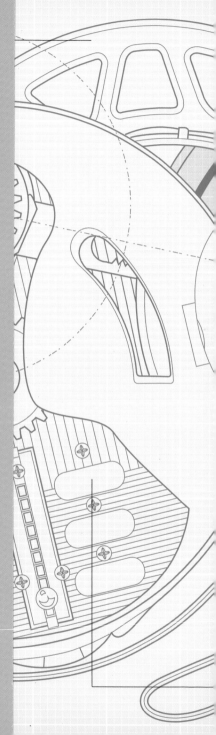

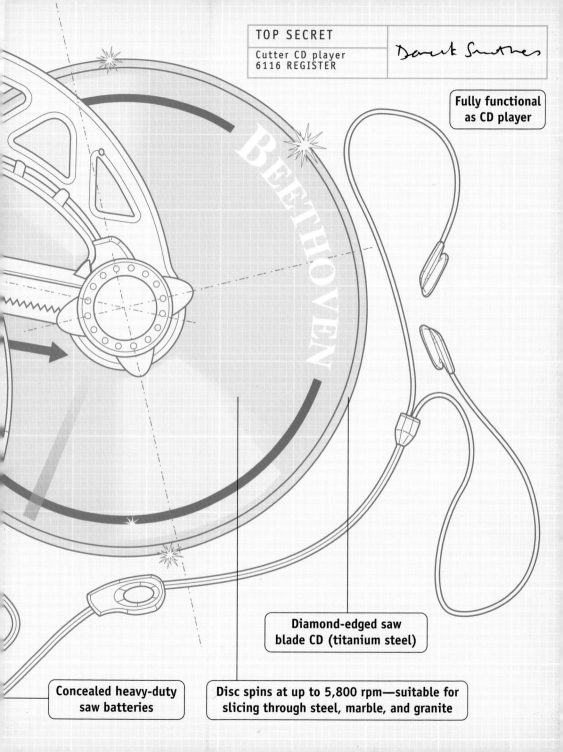

BEETHOVEN

**Fully functional
as CD player**

**Diamond-edged saw
blade CD (titanium steel)**

**Concealed heavy-duty
saw batteries**

**Disc spins at up to 5,800 rpm—suitable for
slicing through steel, marble, and granite**

Multifunction Games Console [1]

The MI6 multifunction games console was developed specially for Alex to take with him to Port Tallon, the home of Herod Sayle's Stormbreaker computer factory. As well as playing games, it was designed to copy documents, set off a smoke bomb, detect bugs, and see through walls.

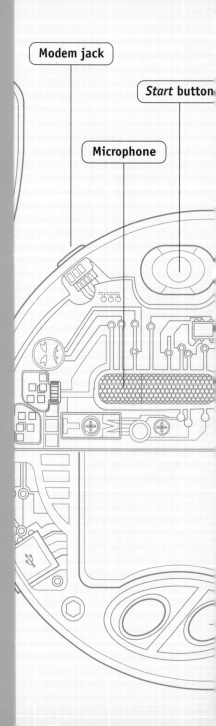

Modem jack

Start button

Microphone

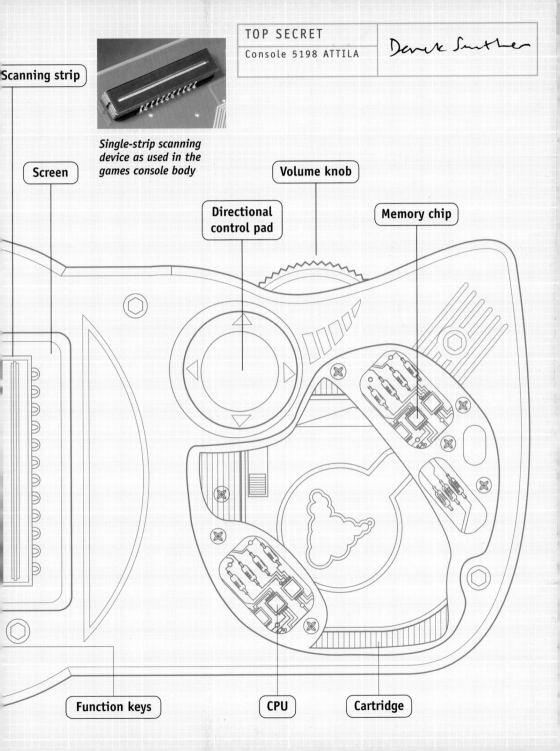

Derek Smithen

Scanning strip

Single-strip scanning device as used in the games console body

Screen

Volume knob

Directional control pad

Memory chip

Function keys

CPU

Cartridge

Multifunction Games Console [2]

Exocet cartridge

Speed Wars cartridge

Bomber Boy cartridge

Nemesis cartridge

Miniature radar chip

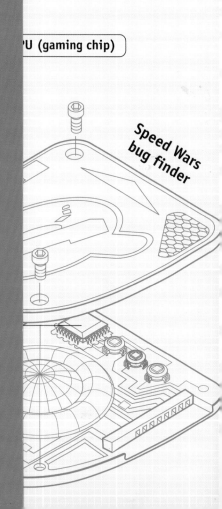

PU (gaming chip)

Speed Wars bug finder

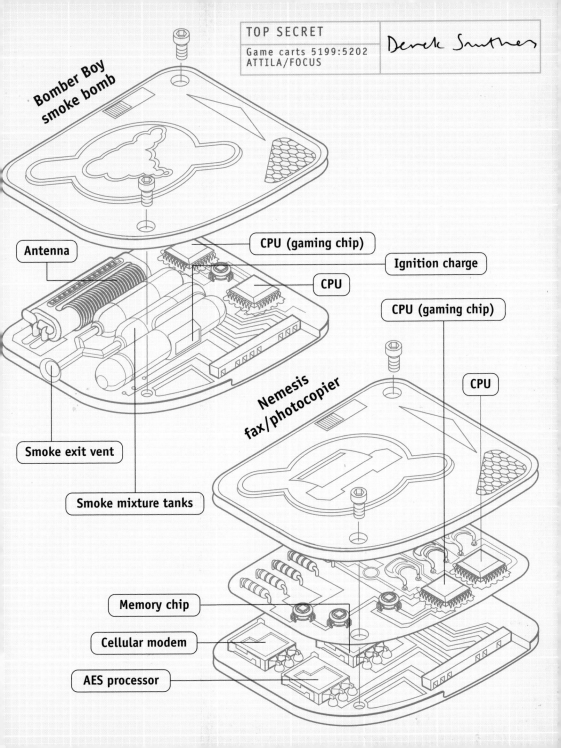

Derek Smithers

Bomber Boy smoke bomb

Antenna

CPU (gaming chip)

Ignition charge

CPU

CPU (gaming chip)

Nemesis fax/photocopier

CPU

Smoke exit vent

Smoke mixture tanks

Memory chip

Cellular modem

AES processor

Geiger Counter Games Console [CIA Issue]

The CIA gave Alex a games console when he went to work for them in Cuba—but what they didn't tell him was that it contained a Geiger counter to help them find a nuclear bomb. Alex discovered its secret function when it picked up the radiation produced by the luminous face on his hotel alarm clock.

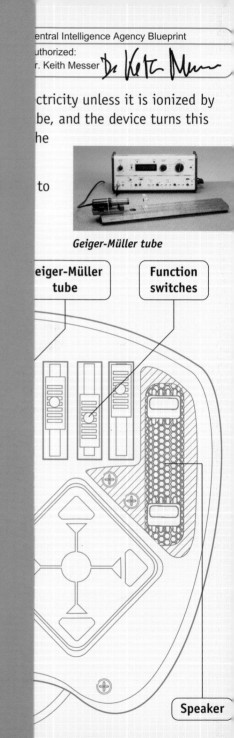

Central Intelligence Agency Blueprint
Authorized:
Dr. Keith Messer

...ctricity unless it is ionized by ...be, and the device turns this ...he

...to

Geiger-Müller tube

Geiger-Müller tube

Function switches

Speaker

MI6 Lab Report [1]

From: Smithers (Covert Weapons Section)
To: C Section; Covert Operations; Archives
Subject: Microcapsules

A recent major breakthrough in MI6's Research and Development section has allowed us to produce some exotic and highly useful new equipment.

We have discovered how to conceal a dangerous substance, such as an acid, poison, or explosive, inside an entirely innocent one. It will pass any sort of inspection short of detailed chemical analysis, and has a better chance of staying in an agent's possession should he or she be captured or searched. Droplets of the substance are sealed inside microscopic capsules, designed to break open only when they come into contact with specific materials; at all other times they are completely harmless.

For example, we took a commonly available ointment used to prevent spots and added microcapsules of a super-acid: an 80% solution of antimony pentafluoride in hydrofluoric acid. On contact with metal, the acid is released by the action of enzymes, and will rapidly eat through most materials. The ointment is perfectly safe for use on the skin, although we recommend that it should not be swallowed, or applied around metal facial piercings.

We are particularly happy with the bubble gum designed for the agent in the Skeleton Key mission. Concealed in the gum are many microcapsules made of starch, which contain a particularly exciting new material: a fullerene foam. When the gum is chewed, the enzyme amylase in saliva breaks down the starch capsules. Fullerene foam is a very strong crystalline lattice of carbon atoms, which expands dramatically on contact with air; placed inside a lock or gun barrel, it will shatter the metal with ease. (Several batches of the gum were produced and tested. We feel the success of the final product justifies the dental bills.)

Other recent uses of this technology include the high explosive contained in a medicated shampoo. Agents should please stop calling it "Head Off Shoulders."

Smithers

Buckminsterfullerene molecule($C60$), a constituent of fullerene foam

High-Tensile Yo-Yo

This high-tech yo-yo was designed to aid climbing—its powerful winch action and strong cord could lift Alex's weight easily. However, not even Smithers could have foreseen how Alex would use it.

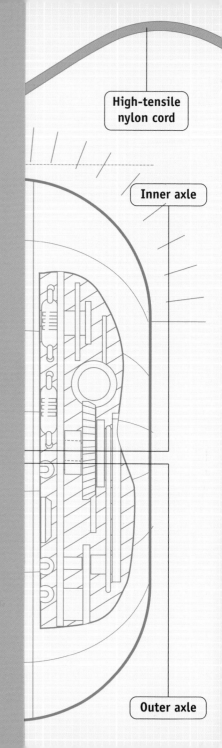

High-tensile nylon cord

Inner axle

Outer axle

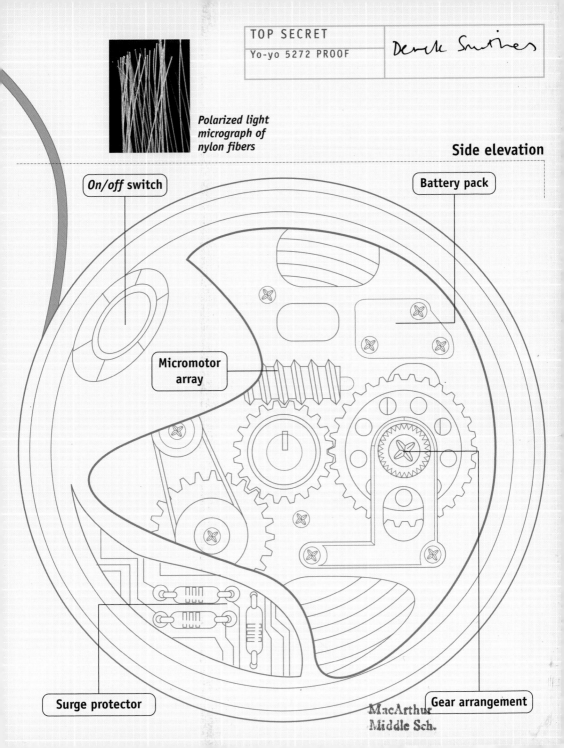

Polarized light
micrograph of
nylon fibers

Side elevation

On/off switch

Battery pack

Micromotor
array

Surge protector

Gear arrangement

MacArthur
Middle Sch.

Infrared Goggles and Bulletproof Ski Suit

Point Blanc Academy was perched on the side of a mountain in the French Alps—so it was only natural that Alex would take a ski suit and a pair of goggles with him. As ever, Smithers had made sure that there was more to them than met the eye.

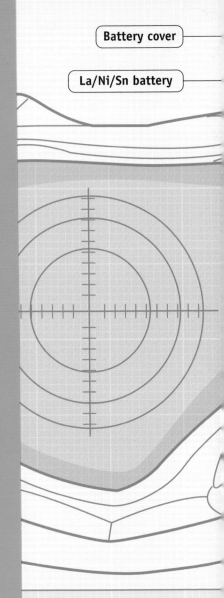

Battery cover

La/Ni/Sn battery

cutting edge of technology, trong material woven from f a human hair, these fibers are silk and seventeen times as ulletproof vests.

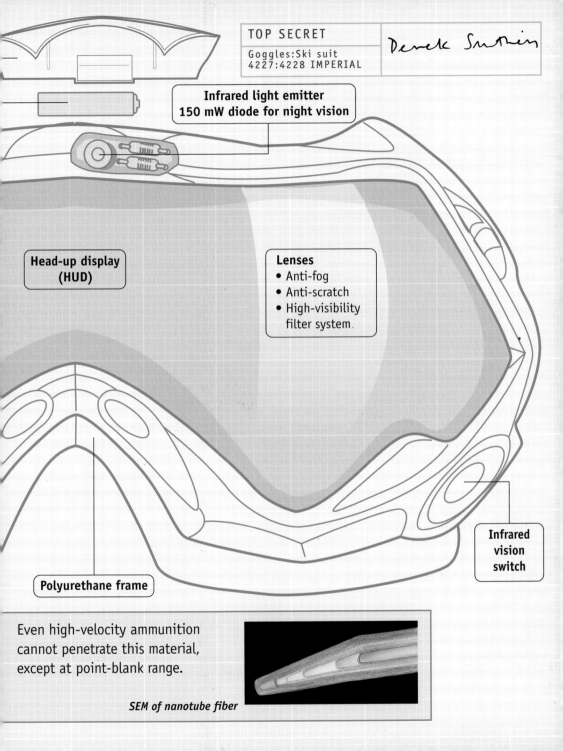

Infrared light emitter
150 mW diode for night vision

Head-up display
(HUD)

Lenses
- Anti-fog
- Anti-scratch
- High-visibility
  filter system.

**Infrared
vision
switch**

Polyurethane frame

Even high-velocity ammunition
cannot penetrate this material,
except at point-blank range.

SEM of nanotube fiber

Exploding Ear Stud

Alex went to Point Blanc Academy pretending to be spoiled rich kid Alex Friend, complete with a pierced ear, a bad reputation, and plenty of attitude. His ear stud, with its hidden charge of explosive, helped him avoid a gruesome fate.

netic
es

ndary arming switch

Lining material
for electric insulation

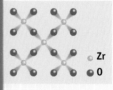

Zr

0

crystal and illustration
ttice

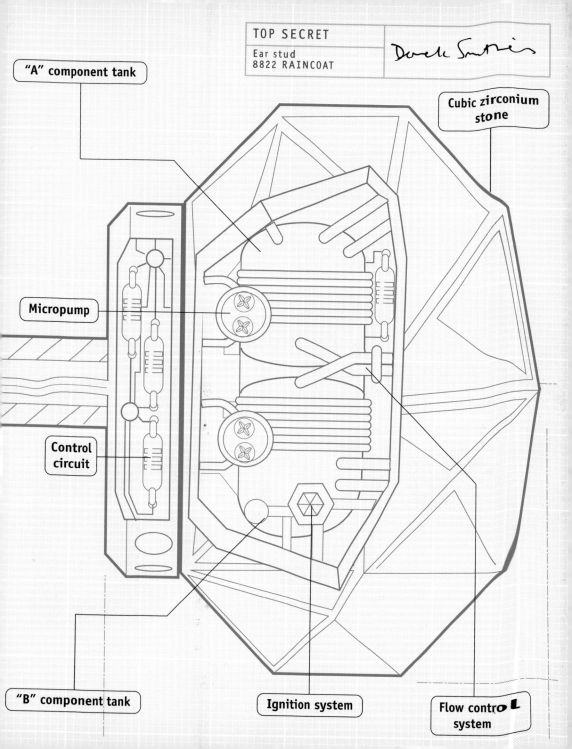

"A" component tank

Cubic zirconium stone

Micropump

Control circuit

"B" component tank

Ignition system

Flow control system

Stun Grenade Key Ring

Stun grenades are used by military and law enforcement units all over the world; they explode in a burst of intense light and noise that incapacitates but does not do any lasting damage. Smithers built one into a novelty key ring shaped like a famous soccer player; it came in very handy for Alex when the clock was ticking in injury time.

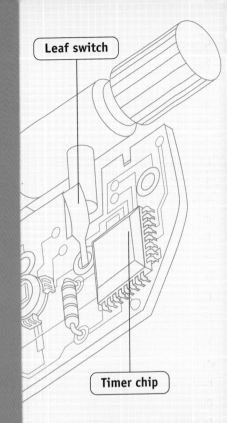

Leaf switch

Timer chip

Explosive combustion of ammonium nitrate

Stun grenade key ring: Known informally as the Striker, this key ring in the shape of a famous soccer player is in fact a stun grenade. When the head of the soccer player is twisted twice clockwise and once counterclockwise, a ten-second fuse is activated. Then a small charge of gunpowder (2.5 grams) detonates, forcing a burst of metallic particles out of concealed holes in the base of the device. The resulting sheet of dust hangs in the air briefly before combining with oxygen and igniting, creating an explosion. This is nonlethal but will effectively stun anybody in a confined space for several minutes.

The metallic dust is made up of 4.5 grams of a pyrotechnic metal-oxidant mix of magnesium and ammonium powder. The particles burn for less than five hundredths of a second, producing a flash of around 2 million candelas and a bang of around 170 decibels. These levels are low enough not to cause blindness or ruptured eardrums.

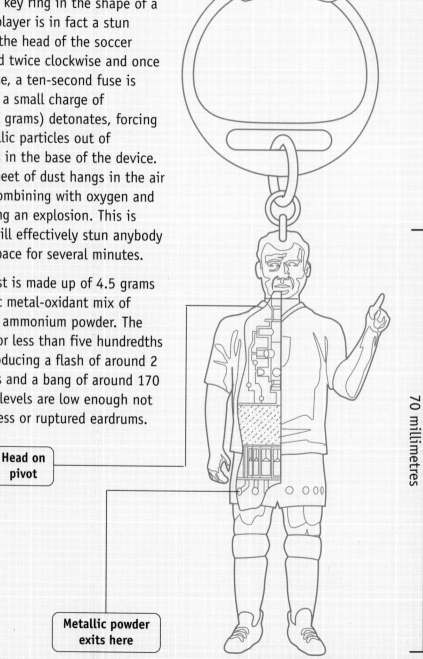

Head on pivot

Metallic powder exits here

70 millimetres

Multifunction Cellular Phone

Alex was sent to work for the CIA—a mission that would take him to Florida, Cuba, and even Russia. Wherever he found himself, he could always contact MI6 using this adapted cellular phone, which works all over the world. The phone is impossible to use unless the agent's fingerprint is detected by the keypad, and Alex's model even contained a hidden tranquilizer dart, which could be fired out of the antenna—and which Alex used to stunning effect.

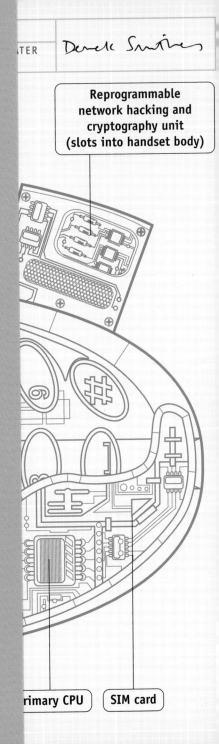

ATER   Derek Smithers

Reprogrammable network hacking and cryptography unit (slots into handset body)

rimary CPU   SIM card

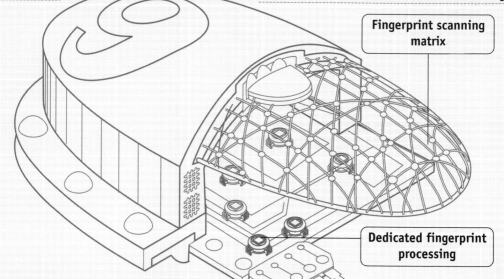

Fingerprint scanning matrix

Dedicated fingerprint processing

Cellular phone [model five]:

This modified cell phone provides a direct link to MI6 headquarters from any location in the world with network service. Sophisticated telephone network hacking routines mean that the calls are untraceable and encrypted to prevent eavesdropping; tracking the phone location is only possible if the correct security codes are known. The entire case, which is made of lightweight, high-impact substances such as titanium steel, ABS resin, and polycarbonate, is sealed and pressurized. It will therefore work underwater to depths of 250 feet and even in the vacuum of space (although the user may have difficulty getting a signal). The phone keypad is fingerprint-sensitive and restricted to the designated user. Unauthorized use is impossible. In the latest versions of the model five, the core of the antenna is in fact a stun dart tipped with RAKO-88, which is shot out by a compressed gas cylinder on dialing 999. The effective range is sixty feet. RAKO-88 causes unconsciousness in a matter of seconds; this lasts up to one hour and has no serious side effects, although headaches and temporary nausea have been reported.

Cellular phone [model seven]: This model has the added features of a mercury switch and a small charge of plastic explosive; unless the phone is held upside down when dialing, it will explode as soon as the call connects.

Stun-Dart Book

Alex is never issued with lethal
weapons on his missions, but
on occasion he needs to be able
to knock an enemy out from a
distance. Smithers designed this
stun-dart book to help him do this
quickly and quietly.

It was a surprise to everyone when
Alex was forced to use it not on
a guard or an assassin, but on a
fifteen-year-old girl.

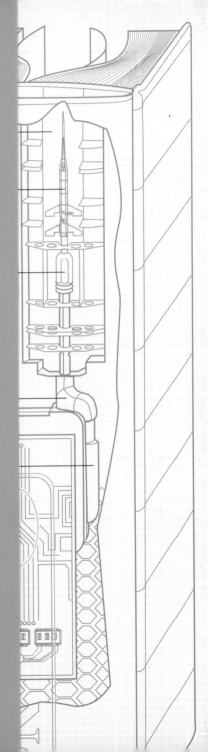

MI6 Lab Report [2]

From: Smithers (Covert Weapons Section)
To: C Section; Covert Operations; Archives
Subject: Project Aegis

Project Aegis was created to research new methods of protecting and assisting staff in embassies and MI6 offices worldwide. The first test systems have been installed in my offices at Liverpool Street and are performing extremely well.

It is vital to be able to check people visiting these offices for weapons and other smuggled material. You may be aware that there is specialized machinery built into the elevators for just that reason. However, we have recently been looking into ultra wideband radar devices that will fit on a desk. The final version, which is disguised as an anglepoise lamp, has been shown to be highly effective. It tracks human beings by body heat, using its millimeter-wavelength radar antenna to detect objects through clothing. The scanner can see all the way through to the human skeleton, and has resolution fine enough to read the text on coins and credit cards. The output can be connected to a PC so that the user can search a guest thoroughly without his or her knowledge.

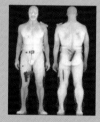

Weapons detection scan

Document security is always a concern. Shredders are bulky and not entirely efficient, so we have researched new methods of destroying papers. The out-tray on my desk contains powerful electric terminals that can disintegrate a document thoroughly in a matter of seconds, with no flame and very little smoke.

Two concealed elevators have been built into my office. One is connected to the Research and Development labs, and the other goes to street level (it comes out in the back room of the Prince of Wales pub, which is handy). The first elevator is built into the large sofa—the middle seat drops into the floor, and the gap is closed by the seats on either side. The second elevator is inside the wall behind the filing cabinet, which splits open to reveal the entrance. We feel this system is ideal for keeping the secure areas of the building secret as well as safe.

Smithers

Cannondale Bad Boy Bike [1]

A bombing in France set Alex on the trail of multimillionaire pop star Damian Cray, but nobody at MI6 would believe him. Nobody, that is, except for Smithers, who sent Alex this modified bicycle—perfect for a chase through the narrow streets of Amsterdam.

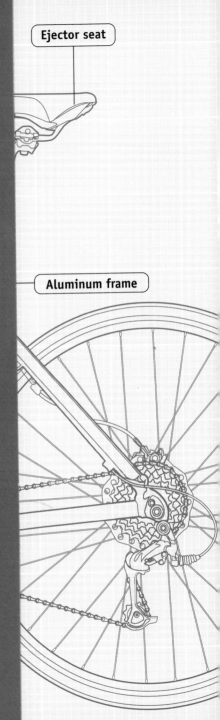

Ejector seat

Aluminum frame

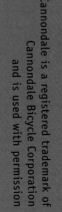

Bike overview: This customized bicycle is designed to provide a fast, safe, and reliable means of transport for agents in urban areas.

The aluminum frame has been engineered to be light, strong, and shock-absorbent; it will stand up to an impressive amount of punishment and is rigid enough to prevent much energy from being wasted through side-to-side movement. State-of-the-art suspension and gearing make for great comfort, speed, and versatility.

The tires, manufactured using a new polyurethane elastomer technology, cannot 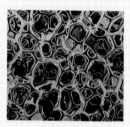 be punctured or lose pressure. The insides contain a honeycomb of pressurized cells that are so small that if one or more deflate, it makes little difference to the performance of the bicycle. They absorb shock and resist weathering more effectively than standard rubber tires.

False color SEM of multicelled polyurethane elastomer

A variety of devices has been built into the bicycle to deter pursuit—a smokescreen, oil dispenser, and two heat-seeking missiles—and the seat post acts as an emergency ejection system. There are also accessories for the rider, such as a bulletproof cycle jersey and magnetic bike clips, and an intensely bright magnesium headlight.

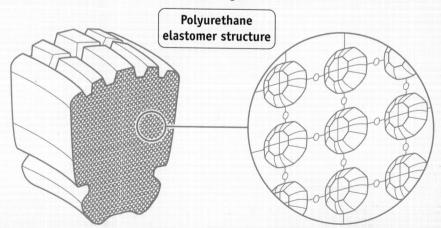

Polyurethane elastomer structure

Cannondale Bad Boy Bike [2]

Bell Control Unit

Handlebar Missile System

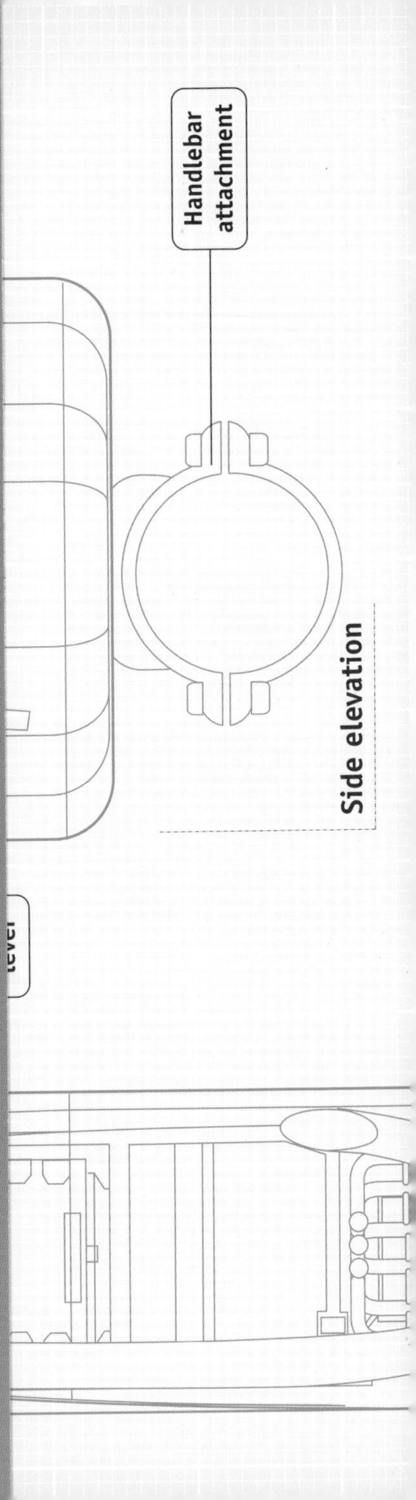

Handlebar attachment

Side elevation

level

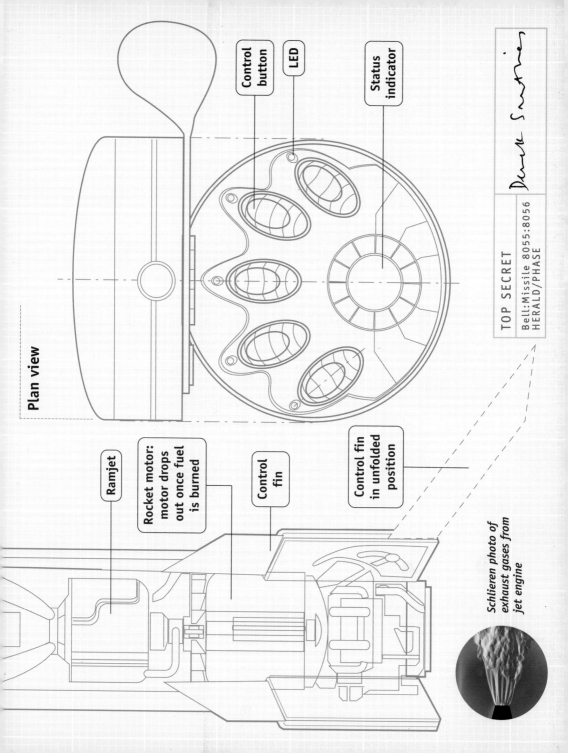

Plan view

Control button

LED

Status indicator

Ramjet

Rocket motor: motor drops out once fuel is burned

Control fin

Control fin in unfolded position

Schlieren photo of exhaust gases from jet engine

TOP SECRET

Bell:Missile 8055:8056
HERALD/PHASE

Cannondale
Bad Boy Bike [3]

Smokescreen
Bike Pump

Ejector Seat

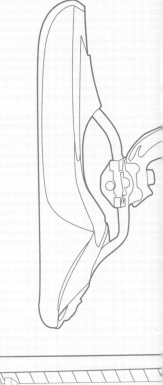

agents are advised to keep this in mind before using the ejection system.

Primary heating coil

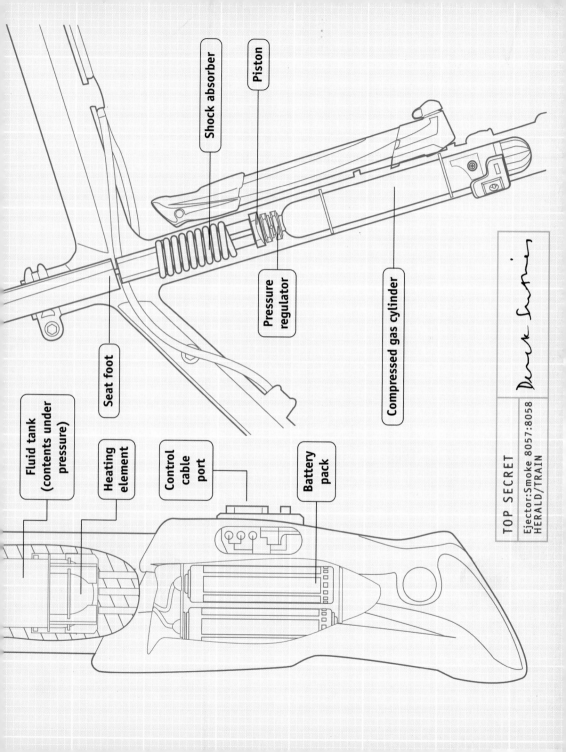

Shock absorber

Piston

Pressure regulator

Compressed gas cylinder

Seat foot

Fluid tank (contents under pressure)

Heating element

Control cable port

Battery pack

TOP SECRET

Ejector:Smoke 8057:8058
HERALD/TRAIN

Cannondale
Bad Boy Bike [4]

Magnesium Flare Headlight

Oil Slick Water Bottle

Magnetic Bike Clips

Bulletproof Cycle Jersey

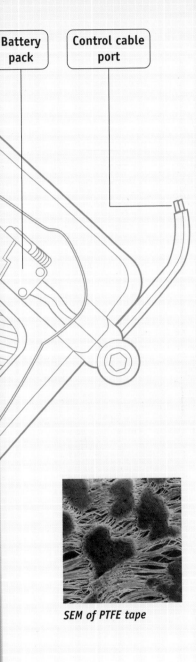

Battery pack

Control cable port

hamber

SEM of PTFE tape

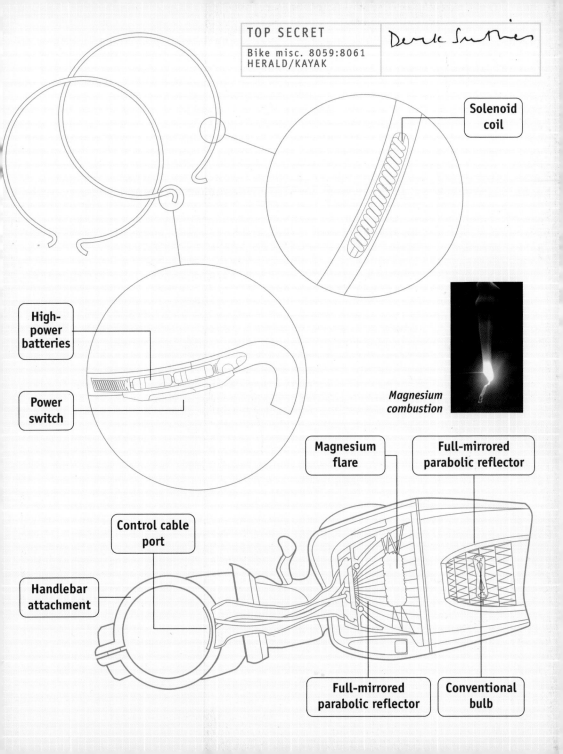

Solenoid
coil

High-
power
batteries

Power
switch

*Magnesium
combustion*

Magnesium
flare

Full-mirrored
parabolic reflector

Control cable
port

Handlebar
attachment

Full-mirrored
parabolic reflector

Conventional
bulb

Radio Mouth Brace

Alex was sent as a double agent to infiltrate the ruthless criminal organization Scorpia. This modified mouth brace, complete with radio transmitter, was designed to allow MI6's strike teams to find him—if he could stay alive long enough.

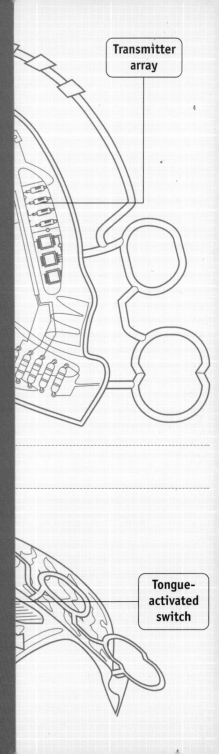

Transmitter array

Tongue-activated switch

Scorpia

From: Smithers (Covert Weapons Section)
To: Everyone, R&D
Subject: Scorpia

You may be aware of the recent activities of the criminal group known as Scorpia. Some of the equipment recently issued to one of their agents is now being researched here at MI6 (documentation follows); here is a brief introduction for those of you who are unfamiliar with this organization.

Taking its name from its four main fields of activity—sabotage, corruption, intelligence and assassination—Scorpia has flourished since it was set up in the early 1980s. It is responsible for a tenth of the world's terrorism, which it undertakes on a contract basis. We suspect its involvement in several major ecological disasters, countless murders, and political manipulation on a massive scale.

Scorpia is led by a small council of ex-government spies and assassins, drawn from the intelligence services of many nations. There were twelve founder members, but now only seven remain. It maintains a training center on the island of Malagosto near Venice, where promising students are taught espionage, survival, and, more importantly, how to kill; a large portion of Scorpia's income comes from contract murders.

Scorpia agents should always be considered armed and dangerous, even after a thorough search, as much of their R&D budget goes on the development of concealed weaponry.

Smithers

Pizza Delivery Assassin Kit [1]

Scorpia sent Alex to kill the deputy head of MI6 Special Operations, Mrs. Jones. He gained access to her heavily guarded apartment building disguised as a pizza delivery boy.

The olives on the four seasons pizza were in fact soundless explosives for destroying locks, and made short work of Mrs. Jones's front door. The guard was already unconscious, a victim of Scorpia's fastest-acting knockout drug, which was administered by a blowgun disguised as a drinking straw.

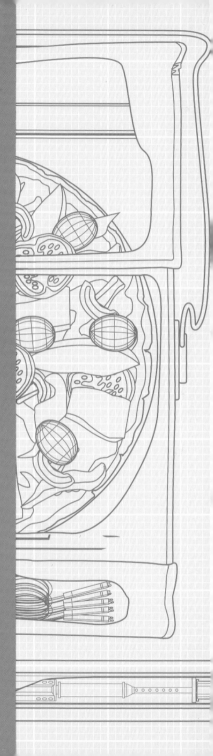

Exploding olives: The olives on the pizza are in fact small thermite charges. The outer shell is thin but tough and flexible; it is made of black plastic disguised to look like a slightly greasy, sticky olive. It contains a small amount of smokeless gunpowder packed around a plastic bag. This bag in turn contains a mixture of powdered aluminum and iron oxide.

A plastic box in the false bottom of the pizza bag contains a piezoelectric crystal similar to those used in gas cigarette lighters; when squeezed, it produces enough current to create a spark. Unlike a battery, it has no metal parts, and so does not risk setting off metal detectors. The very thin metal wires running out of the box should also be undetectable.

The "olives" are stuck and squashed into place and one of the wires is then jabbed through the plastic shell. A button on the capacitor box squeezes the crystal and creates a high-voltage charge through the wires. A spark jumps between the two ends and ignites the smokeless powder. This causes enough heat to start the thermite reaction.

The aluminum and iron oxide mixture burns at a temperature of more than 3,000 degrees Celsius and will cut through any metal in a matter of seconds.

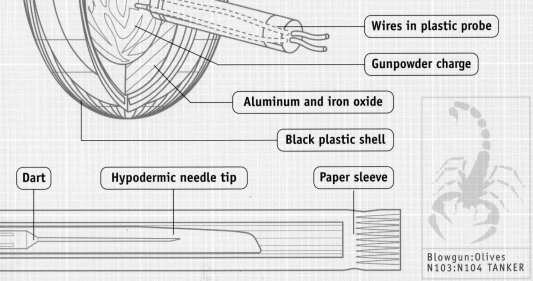

Wires in plastic probe

Gunpowder charge

Aluminum and iron oxide

Black plastic shell

Dart

Hypodermic needle tip

Paper sleeve

Blowgun:Olives
N103:N104 TANKER

Pizza Delivery Assassin Kit [2]

The front entrance to Mrs. Jones's apartment building was guarded by two MI6 agents with a metal detector. In order to smuggle a gun through the sensors, it was concealed inside a bottle of soft drink. Alex had only to leave it on the front desk, step through the detector, and pick it up on the other side.

The special offers card he carried was actually a fake indicator panel for the elevator. Stuck magnetically over the real one, it fooled the agents into thinking that Alex had gone to a different floor.

assignments.

With the bottle assembled and filled, it looks, feels, and weighs almost the same as a real bottle of soft drink; the lid can even be unscrewed and some of the liquid poured out before the package is revealed.

Waterproof bag

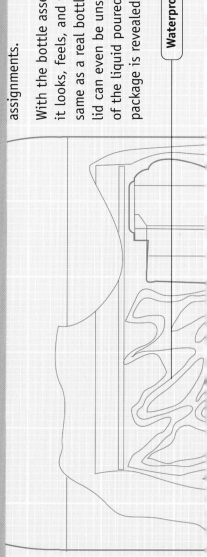

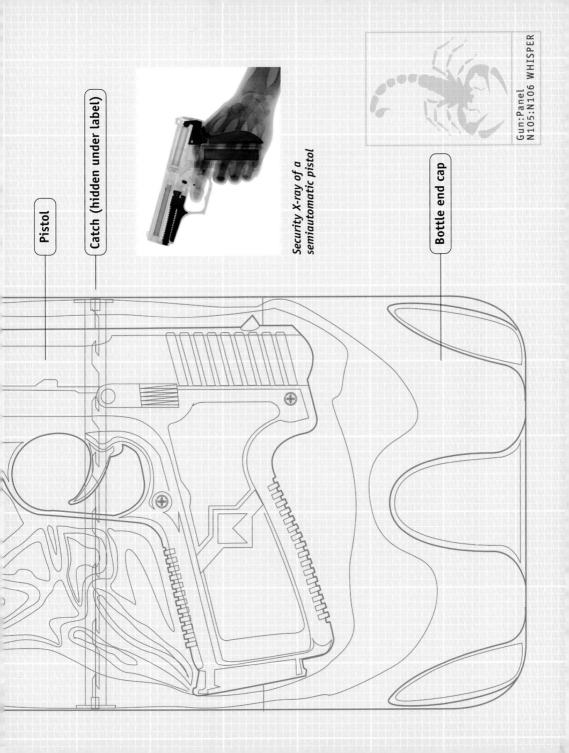

Pistol

Catch (hidden under label)

Security X-ray of a semiautomatic pistol

Bottle end cap

Gun-Panel
N105:N106 WHISPER

Operation Invisible Sword

Scorpia's master plan involved a new and terrifying weapon code-named Invisible Sword. It was based on cutting-edge nanotechnology: a branch of science dealing with objects so small, they can only be seen with scanning electron microscopes. Nanotechnology is already all around us—in windows, car tires, even lipstick—and its widespread use to make weapons as deadly and mysterious as this cannot be far away.

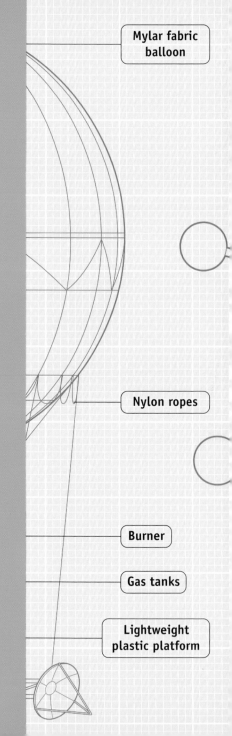

Mylar fabric balloon

Nylon ropes

Burner

Gas tanks

Lightweight plastic platform

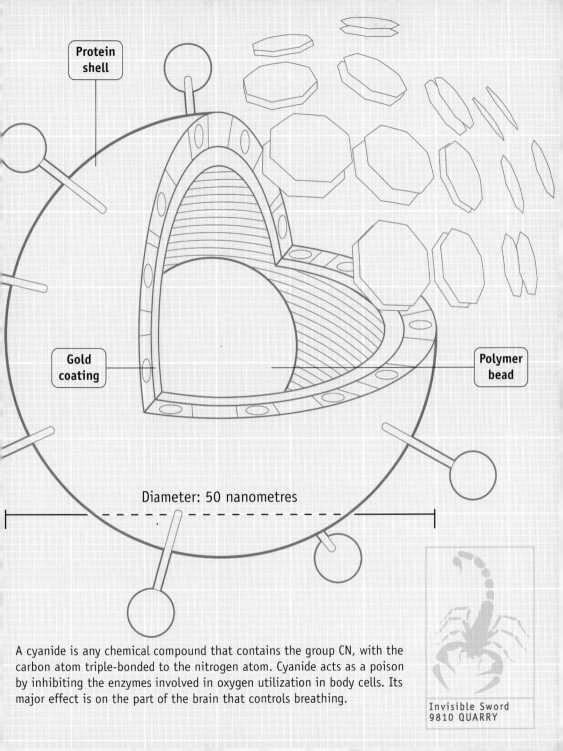

Protein shell

Gold coating

Polymer bead

Diameter: 50 nanometres

A cyanide is any chemical compound that contains the group CN, with the carbon atom triple-bonded to the nitrogen atom. Cyanide acts as a poison by inhibiting the enzymes involved in oxygen utilization in body cells. Its major effect is on the part of the brain that controls breathing.

Invisible Sword
9810 QUARRY

Glossary

Key scientific and technical terms used in this book

ABS resin A type of plastic used to make many different types of products, from pipes to golf-club heads to children's toys. ABS has excellent shock absorbance and is resistant to low temperatures.

Advanced encryption standard (AES) Encryption means making information unreadable unless it is known how to decode it. The advanced encryption standard is a particular way of doing this that has been chosen for use by the United States government; it is considered by experts to be extremely secure, and is relatively easy to use.

Antenna An electronic component designed to send or receive radio waves. Most antennas are simple rods or loops of metal or wire.

Burst transmission A radio transmission that compresses a large amount of information into a short time. Often used by the military to minimize the chance of signals being detected.

Candela (cd) A measure of brightness or intensity of light. An ordinary wax candle produces approximately one candela.

Capacitor A device that stores energy in an electric field. Capacitors can be used like a fast battery and are often used to keep power supply smooth and even.

Central processing unit (CPU) This is the part of a computer that carries out the instructions of the computer program.

Decibel (dB) A measure of sound pressure—often used to describe how loud something is. 10 dB is about as loud as a person's breathing sounds from ten feet away; 80 dB is a vacuum cleaner from one yard; 120 dB is a loud rock concert. At 130 dB, sounds begin to hurt. At 190 dB, they can cause ruptured eardrums, and sounds of 200 dB or more can even kill.

Electromagnet A type of magnet made by passing an electric current through a coil of wire.

Electromagnetic (EM) spectrum The name for the collection of all the different types of EM radiation—waves that carry energy from one place to another. Light is one kind—the only part of the spectrum we can see.

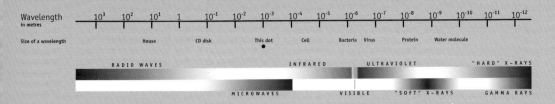

Wavelength in metres 10^3 10^2 10^1 1 10^{-1} 10^{-2} 10^{-3} 10^{-4} 10^{-5} 10^{-6} 10^{-7} 10^{-8} 10^{-9} 10^{-10} 10^{-11} 10^{-12}

Size of a wavelength   House   CD disk   This dot   Cell   Bacteria Virus   Protein   Water molecule

RADIO WAVES   INFRARED   ULTRAVIOLET   "HARD" X-RAYS

MICROWAVES   VISIBLE   "SOFT" X-RAYS   GAMMA RAYS

The spectrum ranges from low-frequency, long-wavelength waves such as radio waves, to microwaves (including terahertz waves), then infrared, visible light (from red through to violet), ultraviolet light, X-rays, and gamma rays (very high-frequency waves) with very short wavelengths.

Enzyme A type of chemical that speeds up chemical reactions. Our bodies contain many different kinds of enzyme to help digest food or to contract and relax our muscles.

Fullerene Amazing though it is, diamond (the hardest mineral known to man) and graphite (the soft substance that makes up pencil leads) are both forms of carbon. The difference is in the shape of the molecules and the way they are bonded together. Fullerene molecules, discovered in the late twentieth century, are atoms of carbon arranged into spheres, tubes or rings.

Geiger counter A device for measuring levels of ionizing radiation—often used for detecting the dangerous radiation given off by the materials used in nuclear reactors and atomic bombs.

Generator A device that turns mechanical energy—such as the spinning of a turbine—into electrical energy.

Head-up display (HUD) Head-up displays, or HUDs, are ways of displaying information to a person in such a way that it is overlaid on what they see, and is always present in their visual field whichever way they look. Jet pilots, for example, can have flight information projected onto their visors, which means they do not have to look away to check their instruments.

High-tensile materials Tension is a force on a material that puts it under strain—a stretching force as opposed to a squeezing force (compression). Tensile strength is a measure of the maximum amount of tension a material can undergo before it breaks. So high-tensile materials can stand large amounts of tension without damage.

Infrared The part of the EM spectrum just below visible light is infrared, which means "below red," just as ultraviolet means "above violet." Objects at room temperature or above emit infrared radiation, emitting more the hotter they are. This cannot be seen with the naked eye, but can be picked up with a special camera or receiver. The many uses for infrared light include night vision equipment (hot objects, like people, will show up more brightly than their surroundings) and remote control units.

Magnesium A silvery-white lightweight metal, magnesium ignites when exposed to air and burns with a dazzling white flame.

Mercury switch Mercury is a metal that is liquid at room temperature. In a mercury tilt switch, a blob of the metal is contained in a glass bulb. At either end, there is a pair of electrical contacts. If the switch is tilted, and mercury rolls down to either end, it will complete the circuit.

Nanofiber Fibers made from tiny carbon nanotubes—rolled-up sheets of graphite fifty thousand times thinner than a human hair. Some types of nanofiber are thought to be the world's toughest material.

Nanotechnology One nanometer is one millionth of a millimeter. Scientists have recently begun thinking about machines of around this scale— from 0.1 to 100 nanometers. Some simple machines have already been made, including gears and motors.

Nylon A strong, flexible type of plastic often made into fibers and ropes.

Piezoelectric effect Certain crystals, when squeezed, produce an electrical voltage. This effect is also reversible; applying an electrical voltage to the crystal can cause it to change shape slightly. Some cigarette lighters use a piezoelectric crystal—it is squeezed to provide the electric spark that lights the gas. Quartz crystals in many watches and clocks use this effect to create a series of pulses, keeping the clock ticking regularly.

Plastic explosive Developed shortly before the Second World War, plastic explosives are soft, easy to mold into shape, and are safe over a wider range of temperatures than other explosives.

Polycarbonate A tough, durable form of plastic that can be molded once heated up. Products made from it include sunglasses lenses, compact discs, and even bulletproof glass.

Polytetrafluoroethylene (PTFE) A material that is often used as a nonstick coating for pans and other cookware. It has the lowest coefficient of friction of any solid substance known to man—which is another way of saying that it is very slippery.

Polyurethane elastomer A rubbery material containing many tiny cells.

Radioactivity Some materials—called radioactive isotopes—decay naturally over time, giving off various particles or rays in the process. This radiation can be extremely dangerous to living creatures as it can destroy or alter the cells of the body. Radioactive isotopes such as uranium-235 and plutonium-239 are used in nuclear weapons.

Ramjet A type of jet engine designed to work at very high speeds, so that air is forced into the front of the engine; ramjets do not work well at speeds of less than six hundred miles per hour. They are lightweight and contain no major moving parts.

Scanning electron micrograph (SEM)
An ordinary microscope works by bouncing a beam of light off the object being studied; a scanning electron microscope uses a beam of electrons. Because electrons have a much shorter wavelength, it is able to see much finer detail. Some of the pictures in this book have been taken in this way, and so are referred to as scanning electron micrographs.

Schlieren photography A method for photographing the flow of air (or other compressible fluids) around objects. It is useful in aircraft or car design to help make the vehicle aerodynamic.

Solar panels Devices that convert light into electricity.

Terahertz waves One hertz means "once per second"; one terahertz means "one thousand billion times per second." Terahertz waves are high-frequency radio waves, similar to microwaves, which cycle one thousand billion times a second.

Thermite reaction A chemical reaction, involving aluminum and (usually) iron oxide, which produces intense heat.

Titanium A metal which is as strong as steel but 45% lighter, and highly resistant to corrosion. Often mixed with other metals to form titanium alloys, it is used in the manufacture of aircraft, missiles, and everyday products such as golf clubs and bicycles.

Universal serial bus (USB)
USB cables and ports are a common way of connecting modern computer devices, such as mice, printers, and cameras, to computers.

Ultra wideband (UWB) radar
A type of radar that can be used to see through walls; it is being developed for use by the military and the police.

Collect all the Alex Rider™ Adventures:

STORMBREAKER

 POINT BLANK

SKELETON KEY

 EAGLE STRIKE

SCORPIA

ARK ANGEL